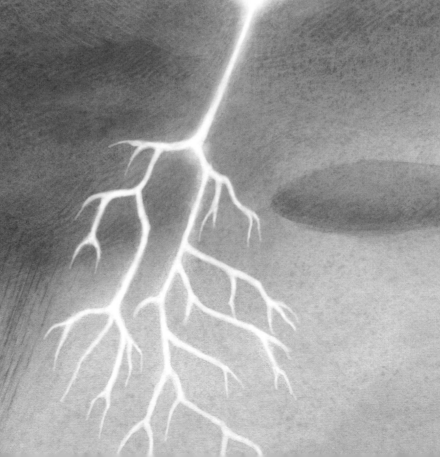

THE END IS JUST THE BEGINNING

written by
Mike Bender

illustrated by
Diana Mayo

Crown Books for Young Readers
New York

THE END.

That's right.
You read it correctly.
You've reached the end . . .
and the beginning.

But wait—how can a book possibly start
with the end? That's ridiculous.

Well, prepare to have your mind blown,
because **the end** isn't really the end.
It's just **the beginning** of something else!

Like this beautiful sunset.
Sure seems like the end
of the day, right?

Not so fast.
You see, when the sun goes down,
it's actually just
the beginning of the night.

When all the snow melts
at the end of winter,
that just means it's
the beginning of spring.

is one big circle.

going back to the beginning because the Earth

If you try to go to the ends of the Earth, you'll actually just keep

If you blast off in a rocket ship,
you'll reach the end of the sky . . .

otherwise known as
the beginning of outer space.

When you count, the end of one number is just the beginning of the next number . . .

and so on and so on and so on, all the way to infinity, which, by the way, NEVER ends!

Even a sign that literally says Dead End isn't an end at all.

It's only just the beginning
of whatever lies beyond it.

So, when you really think about it,
the end . . . is entirely endless.

The end of a disagreement with someone . . .

is just the beginning of making up.

The end of a mistake . . .
is just the beginning
of learning something new.

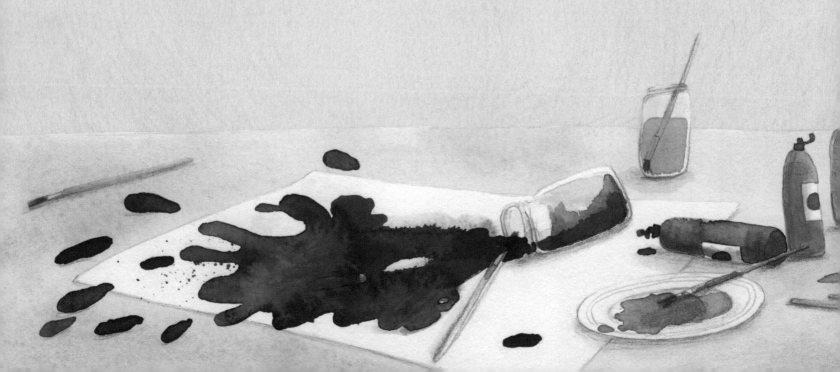

The end of being sick . . .

is just the beginning of
feeling better.

The end of dinner . . .
is just the beginning of dessert.

And if you're really well behaved, the end of dessert
might just be the beginning of MORE dessert!

So tonight, when you turn off
the lights and go to bed,
don't think of it as the end
of anything.

Just think of it as the
beginning of a new tomorrow
full of possibilities!

THE BEGINNING
(of discovering the next book)

To SuChin, Kai, and Soe.
There's nobody else I would rather
end my nights and begin my days with.
—M.B.

For Jake,
with whom I'm still enjoying new beginnings
—D.M.

Text copyright © 2021 by Mike Bender
Jacket art and interior illustrations copyright © 2021 by Diana Mayo

All rights reserved. Published in the United States by Crown Books for Young Readers,
an imprint of Random House Children's Books, a division of Penguin Random House LLC, New York.

Crown and the colophon are registered trademarks of Penguin Random House LLC.

Visit us on the Web! rhcbooks.com

Educators and librarians, for a variety of teaching tools, visit us at RHTeachersLibrarians.com

Library of Congress Cataloging-in-Publication Data
Names: Bender, Mike, author. | Mayo, Diana, illustrator.
Title: The end is just the beginning / Mike Bender ; illustrated by Diana Mayo.
Description: First edition. | New York : Crown Books for Young Readers, [2021] | Audience: Ages 3–7. | Audience: Grades K–1. |
Summary: A caterpillar introduces the concept that each ending is the beginning of something else,
as when the end of a day marks the beginning of night.
Identifiers: LCCN 2020010670 (print) | LCCN 2020010671 (ebook) | ISBN 978-1-9848-9693-3 (hardcover) |
ISBN 978-1-9848-9694-0 (library binding) | ISBN 978-1-9848-9695-7 (ebook)
Subjects: CYAC: Perception—Fiction.
Classification: LCC PZ7.1.B4528 End 2021 (print) | LCC PZ7.1.B4528
(ebook) | DDC [E]—dc23

The text of this book is set in 20-point Bauer Bodoni.
The illustrations in this book were created using acrylic paint, colored pencil, and collage.
Book design by Nicole de las Heras

MANUFACTURED IN CHINA

10 9 8 7 6 5 4 3 2 1

First Edition

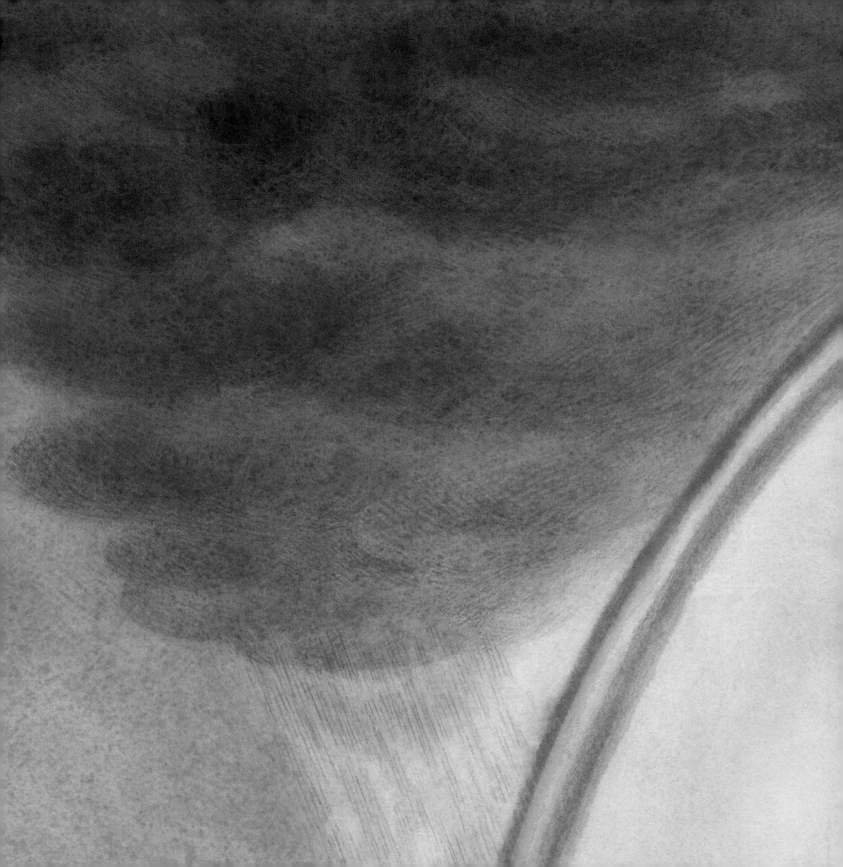